CW01024255

For Gaffer – CdV

For Mom and Dad

Thank you for your love and encouragement – CN

Published by Struik Nature
(an imprint of Random House Struik (Pty) Ltd)
Reg. No. 1966/003153/07
Wembley Square, First Floor, Solan Road, Gardens, Cape Town, 8001
PO Box 1144, Cape Town, 8000 South Africa

Visit **www.randomstruik.co.za** and join the
Struik Nature Club for updates, news, events and special offers.

First published in 2013 by Struik Nature
1 3 5 7 9 10 8 6 4 2

Copyright © in text, 2013: Charles de Villiers
Copyright © in illustrations, 2013: Claire Norden
Copyright © in published edition, 2013: Random House Struik (Pty) Ltd
Reproduction by Hirt & Carter Cape (Pty) Ltd
Printed and bound by Toppan Leefung Printing Limited

All rights reserved. No part of this publication may be
reproduced, stored in a retrieval system, or transmitted, in any
form or by any means, electronic, mechanical, photocopying,
recording or otherwise, without the prior written
permission of the copyright owner(s).

ISBN 978 1 77584 067 1
ePUB: 978 1 77584 084 8
ePDF: 978 1 77584 083 1

Ook in Afrikaans beskikbaar as *Die Vernuftige Verkleurmannetjie*
ISBN 978 1 77584 068 8

Curly the Chameleon

Charles de Villiers

Illustrated by Claire Norden

This bush in the garden with leaves green and flat
Seems to have nothing in it, not even a gnat.

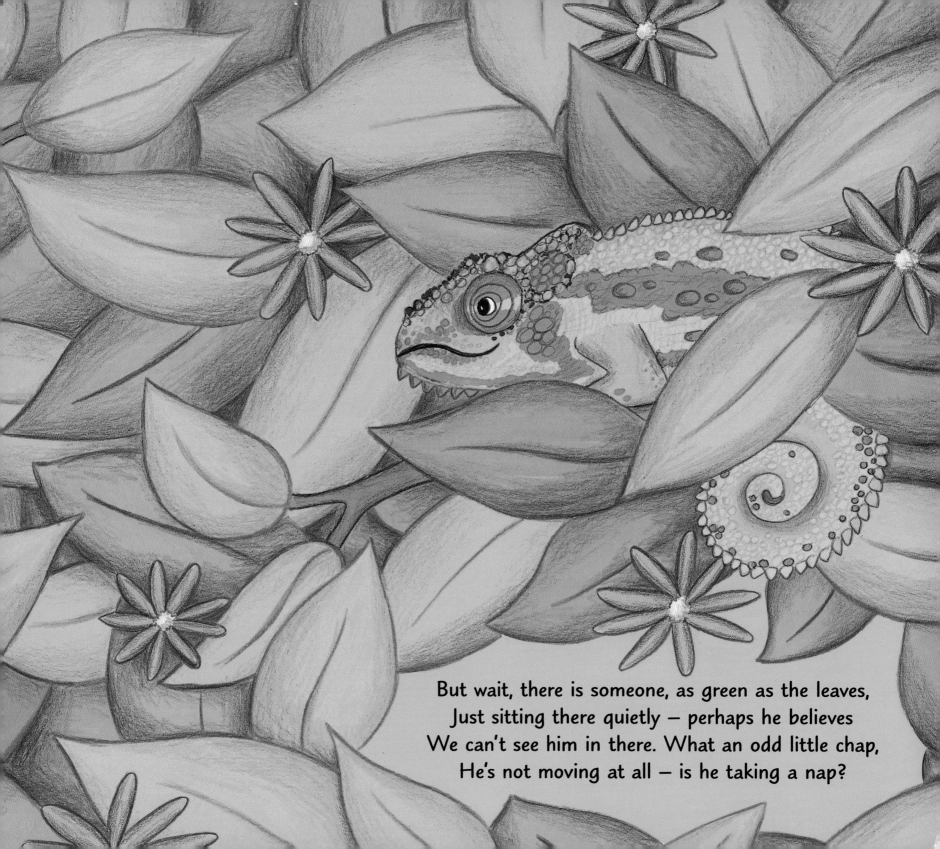

But wait, there is someone, as green as the leaves,
Just sitting there quietly — perhaps he believes
We can't see him in there. What an odd little chap,
He's not moving at all — is he taking a nap?

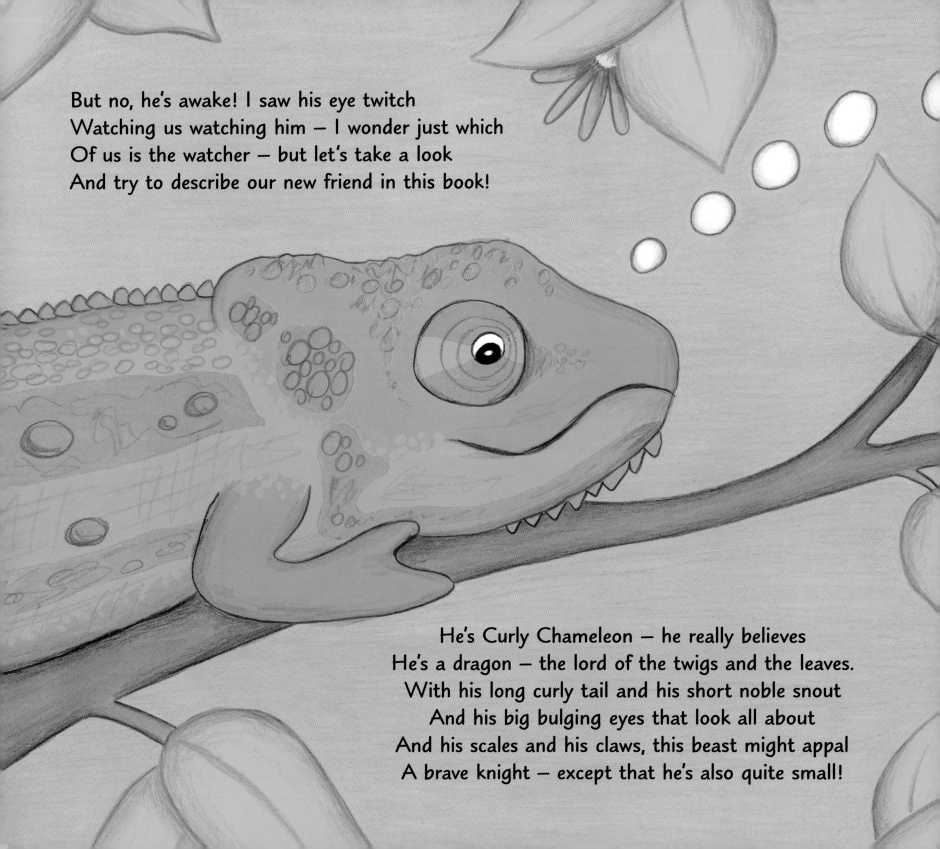

But no, he's awake! I saw his eye twitch
Watching us watching him — I wonder just which
Of us is the watcher — but let's take a look
And try to describe our new friend in this book!

He's Curly Chameleon — he really believes
He's a dragon — the lord of the twigs and the leaves.
With his long curly tail and his short noble snout
And his big bulging eyes that look all about
And his scales and his claws, this beast might appal
A brave knight — except that he's also quite small!

He's not quite as big as the palm of your hand.
But if you were an insect, you'd soon understand
That Curly's a monster – a mythical beast
Who would gladly devour a large fly for a feast!

His eyes are on turrets that swivel about,
While one scans the leaves, the other looks out
For food, any insects and specially flies,
And watches for danger. Perhaps from the skies!

He's got spines on his back in a great spiky arc
And a greeny-brown-grey mottled skin that goes dark
When he's frightened. His tail's wound up tight like a spring,
But it's longer than he is — that's quite a thing!

He's covered with tubercles, soft little bumps
That are sometimes spaced widely and sometimes make clumps.
His beard is all knobbly, his face looks quite stern —
If he wasn't so small he could give you a turn!

He's spotted a fly! Now it buzzes and teases,
As it circles and hovers and rides on the breezes.
Not a care in the world has this bothersome fly,
It's quite unaware of the swivelling eye!

It lands on a flower, and preens its gauze wings,
As it savours the scent of the petals and things.
Our hero takes aim, he measures the gap,
You'd think it's too far — but then, with a ZAP!
His tongue lashes out — grabs the fly from the flower,
Whips back in a flash — then he can devour
His prize. It's delicious! The fly's fresh and sweet,
A juicy and crunchy chameleon treat!

But while he's enjoying his afternoon snack
He keeps a look out, scanning round front and back
With his marvellous eyes. Just a minute — what's that?
He's seen a small movement — the neighbourhood cat!

Now cats are chameleons' most dangerous foes.
They'll eat a chameleon, right down to his toes.
And a cat looks quite huge to chameleon eyes —
Just as big as chameleons look, to the flies.

What to do? Well, chameleons know a few tricks,
And Curly has ways to get out of a fix.
He stops chewing away on the fly in his jaws,
And tightens his grip on the twig with his claws.
If you can't run away, then the very best plan
Is to hide in plain sight, stay as still as you can.
His tail wraps itself round a neighbouring branch.
And in this big crisis, where many might blanch,

Our hero gets *darker*; his skin takes a hue
That's far from its regular yellowy-blue
And greeny-brown-grey — instead, it just fades
Into gloomy-brown royal-blue-charcoaly shades.
You might think that those colours aren't too hard to see;
But they blend in so well with the branch of the tree
And its mouldy old bark, that from down on the ground
It looks as if Curly's no longer around!

Cat narrows his eyes — he's sure he saw food
But now it's *just gone* — and that ruins his mood.
He grumpily twitches his tail once or twice
And then wanders off to go hunting for mice.

Curly heaves a chameleon's sigh of relief:
He's outwitted the cat, the destroyer-in-chief!
He's really quite pleased with himself, is our Curly.
He thinks that he might treat himself to an early
Light lunch — but he's bored with just waiting around
For the flies to appear. If he climbed up and found
Some tasty new insects high up in the tree,
What a juicy and well-earned reward that would be!

So Curly sets off — chameleons aren't quick,
And he's quite a strange sight as he creeps up the stick
With his slow, jerky walk and his hesitant way.
But Curly believes he's a hero today,
He thinks, "I've outsmarted the Lion of the garden,
The King of the suburbs!" Perhaps we can pardon
His pride — but our hero is not looking out
As he should be, for danger — and danger's about!

Look up! There's a dark little speck in the sky
And it's fast growing bigger — I'm sure you know why —
It's a bird! It's a hawk! And it's swooping down low
'Cause it's seen the chameleon moving below.
It's too late for Curly to hide — he's been spotted,
And he can't run away — he's never once trotted;
Still less can he gallop, or scurry, or flee —
Chameleons simply can't do that, you see.

Oh no! The hawk's got him! He's caught in its claws,
And he's whisked in the air as the hawk flaps, then soars
High over the garden. As Curly looks down
He can see the next house and the road into town!
He's terrified now — but he knows he must fight
With all of his strength; so he tries hard to bite
At the claws that are holding him fast in their grip,
And he lashes his tail like a tiny green whip.

He wriggles and writhes, and he struggles like crazy.
The hawk's very strong, but a little bit lazy;
While thinking of supper, he loosens his grip
Just a bit as he turns, and he lets Curly slip!

Our hero is free! But he's ever so high,
And chameleons just weren't intended to fly.
Luckily Curly's a light little chap,
Though he doesn't have wings and he surely can't flap.

He doesn't fall quite like a stone or a rock,
But more like a feather, or maybe a sock.

So he falls rather gently, and lands on a bough,
Which he grapples and grasps, gets his footing somehow,
Then catches his breath, takes a good look around
And decides that in future he'll stay near the ground.

Even so, when his grandchildren sit at his knee,
And ask if he's ever forsaken the tree,
He'll tell of the day he rose into the blue
And fought with the hawk, like a dragon — then flew!